LOOK OUT FOR THE WHOLE SERIES!

THE CASE OF THE
MEDIEVAL MEATHEAD

**Hodder
Children's
Books**

A division of Hachette Children's Books

Special thanks to Lucy Courtenay and Artful Doodlers

Copyright © 2008 Chorion Rights Limited, a Chorion company

First published in Great Britain in 2008 by Hodder Children's Books

1

A Catalogue record for this book is available from the British Library

ISBN 978 0 340 95982 4

Typeset in Weiss by Avon DataSet Ltd,
Bidford on Avon, Warwickshire

Printed in Great Britain by
Clays Ltd, St Ives plc

The paper and board used in this paperback by Hodder Children's
Books are natural recyclable products made from wood grown in
sustainable forests. The manufacturing processes conform to the
environmental regulations of the country of origin.

Hodder Children's Books
a division of Hachette Children's Books
338 Euston Road, London NW1 3BH
An Hachette Livre UK Company
www.hachettelivre.co.uk

Chapter One

The morning sun flooded the beautiful tree-covered island. Wispy white clouds scudded through the perfectly blue sky. On a hill above the harbour, a magnificent castle spread its crenellated shadow across a collection of brightly coloured, medieval-style tents. Pennants fluttered in the breeze.

"Avalon Island," Jo declared. "An idyllic weekend for the whole family."

"And a wicked trip back in time to the thrill-filled Middle Ages!" Max said approvingly.

Inside one of the colourful tents, a young man wearing a crown and doublet and holding a sceptre was waving regally to assembled onlookers. A pretty, long-haired young woman in an elegant medieval dress was smiling on his arm.

"Home to the noble King Oliver," Jo continued, "the fair Princess Petula . . ."

"And the Dark Prince Roland!" Max added.

They all stared at the young man with dark hair, wearing a suit of armour with a wooden sword at his side, who was glowering at King Oliver as he raised a golden goblet in salute.

Timmy the dog took a long, appreciative sniff at Prince Roland.

"It sounds so fun," Allie said, peering over her cousins' shoulders as they all stared at the glossy holiday brochure in Jo's hands. "I can't wait to go. Let's see, I'll need my scrunchies, my travel make-up case—"

"We have to live just like they did in the Middle Ages," tomboy Jo reminded her looks-obsessed cousin with a grin. "No make-up."

"Oh," Allie said. She pulled a face. "I'm not going."

Max looked at Allie from beneath his shaggy blond fringe. The fringe made him look like a dog that was after a treat. "But that's the fun of it!" he

2

said. "It's all old-school. Being chivalrous, eating turkey legs, wiping your hands off on the dog . . ."

Timmy withdrew his nose from the brochure and retreated to a safe distance.

"Probably no computers," Dylan said dismissively. Computers were Dylan's world. "No wonder they called it the Dark Ages."

Allie was looking interested again. "But they did have princesses, right?" she checked. Princesses were big in California. "Ooh, I can be a princess! OK, I'll go – it'll be fun."

"Fun?!" Dylan snorted, looking unimpressed.

"Try dull. Nothing exciting ever happened in the Middle Ages."

Back on Avalon Island, King Oliver, Princess Petula and Prince Roland were drinking a toast from their goblets. Suddenly, Prince Roland dropped his goblet and staggered forward. His face turned pale. He grabbed his throat, gurgled frantically and toppled to the floor. Stone dead . . .

Chapter Two

King Oliver and Princess Petula stared in horror at the lifeless body of Prince Roland. Then King Oliver began to clap.

"Bravo!" called King Oliver as Prince Roland opened his eyes and Princess Petula helped him to his feet. "An excellent performance!"

"Totally believable," Princess Petula gushed. "You didn't move a muscle."

King Oliver looked delighted. "This is going to be our best, most convincing, most mysterious murder mystery weekend ever!" he declared, getting to his feet. "Come on," he summoned the rest of his court, "time to greet our audience . . ."

Down on the jetty, in the selfsame castle shadows that the Five had seen in the brochure, a passenger boat was docking. A round-faced, plump-hipped police officer stepped on to the gangplank and looked dreamily at the romantic scene unfolding before her.

"Avalon Island," Constable Stubblefield murmured, her eyes blazing with happy anticipation. "Three days to be the gentle maiden I was born to be." She strode down the gangplank. "Step aside, my lads," she commanded, elbowing two large gentlemen out of her way and knocking them off the gangplank and into the water. "I'm off to pick posies."

Two dark-haired teenagers were next to appear. They looked very much alike, with identical expressions of disgust on their chiselled, spoiled features.

"Avalon Island ruled by someone else?" said Blaine Dunston, hardly able to believe his own ears. "Ridiculous. We should be King and Queen of this island."

Blaine's sister Daine turned to the puffing servant staggering down the gangplank behind them with his arms full of expensive luggage. "Crawford?" Daine commanded. "Rouse the peasants and organize a rebellion immediately."

"We just got here and the Dunstons are already revolting," Allie sighed as the Five emerged from the boat and made their way ashore.

"Let's be fair," Dylan said reasonably. "They're *always* revolting."

The assorted passengers from the boat gathered on the jetty. A dramatic fanfare drew their attention up to a rocky cliff, where a gangly, hapless youth in a pageboy's brightly coloured doublet and hose was raising a medieval trumpet to his lips. He trilled out another fanfare, then lowered his trumpet nervously. His Adam's apple bobbed in his throat like a cork in a rough sea.

"Pray silence," he squeaked, "for the good and noble King Olive Oil." He paused, looking worried. "Oliver," he amended quickly. "King Oliver! . . . *Come on, Edwin*," he muttered under his breath, *"focus! Idiot!"*

King Oliver appeared on the ramparts, waving royally as he addressed the goggling passengers below. "Good morrow, friends!" he declared. "Let the kettle drum to the trumpet bray, the king and guests do take their rout!"

"Could you repeat that in English please?" Allie asked after a beat of silence.

"It *is* English," Jo hissed. "It means 'hello'."

The passengers murmured together in excitement, and a cry of "Hurrah!"was heard.

The king's expression changed. He leaned against the ramparts as he addressed the wide-eyed crowd below. "But be thou warned," he said, lowering his voice dramatically, "for a crime will be committed this day and it is your duty to discover who the culprit i—"

The sound of splintering wood filled the air. The ramparts gave way, revealing an inner skeleton of wood and canvas as King Oliver pitched forward. The gangly Squire Edwin tried to grab the king – but he too lost his balance. Both of them tumbled over the broken rampart and rolled down to the edge of the cliff. Before the shocked gaze of the crowds, they fell over the edge, leaving King Oliver clinging on by his fingertips and Squire Edwin clinging to the king.

As the king's crown fell and landed at the feet of

the Five, they shared a quick look. Then they raced forward, scrambling up the cliffside path with Timmy leading the way.

"This is so exciting!" Constable Stubblefield squealed. She reached out and caught Squire Edwin's trumpet as it spiralled down from the cliff. "You'd swear it was real!"

To the sound of the police officer improvising a triumphant fanfare down below, King Oliver's grip on the springy cliff grass started to slip. Just in time, a hand grabbed on to his wrist. Then another. Then two more. The Five heaved King Oliver and Squire Edwin to safety. Squire Edwin covered the solid ground with kisses of relief.

"Thank thee, good subjects," King Oliver panted, patting himself down and turning to stare up at the fake wall above them.

"Syrup – I mean, *sire*— "Squire Edwin gabbled, "that fall wasn't in the script."

"No fear, Squire," said King Oliver. "Accidents happen."

The King left the Five with a further nod of thanks. Squire Edwin crawled off after him.

"Constable Stubblefield doesn't realize how

right she is," Max said, as he and Dylan inspected the broken rampart. "This was real. This strut's been sawn through."

"We have a *real* mystery on our hands," Jo announced. The thrill of the challenge gleamed in her dark brown eyes. "Let us hie hence to yon fair burg."

The others looked perplexed.

"Let's get to the village," Jo translated with a sigh.

Chapter Three

As with the rest of the island, Avalon village was like something out of a fairy tale.

A circle of tents with stalls set up in front of them were selling medieval wares such as wooden swords, musical instruments, armorial shields and crowns. The tourist crowd milled around, dazed by the pageantry of it all.

Fully kitted out for their medieval adventure, the Five strode into the village. Allie was wearing an ornate medieval dress and a long, braided wig. Max clanked along in a suit of armour, a wooden sword and shield by his side. A pleased-looking Dylan was dressed as a wealthy merchant with a gold chain, while a less pleased-looking Jo stomped along in a flowing dress and conical princess hat.

"Let's split up and investigate," Jo said, wriggling uncomfortably in her dress as Max chomped through a turkey leg with every sign of enjoyment. "Look for anyone who could have set up King Oliver's 'accidental' fall."

Dylan eyed Jo's dress. It was weird seeing his cousin in something other than combats. "Maybe we should investigate," he teased, "and you should wait in a tower for a prince to rescue you, Miss Pointy Hat."

Jo scowled. "I don't know why they stuck me in a dress," she said bitterly.

"It's the Middle Ages," Allie soothed. "They didn't make armour in Junior Miss sizes."

The lanky Squire Edwin approached them, five small leather sacks in his arms. "Greetings, travellers, and fair time of day," he said, in a wooden attempt at medieval-speak. "I bring pelf."

"Hey, pelf! He brings pelf!" said Max, looking pleased. "What's pelf?"

"It's money," Dylan said in a reverent voice.

The others looked at Dylan in surprise. For

someone so anti-Middle Ages, he had the lingo off pat.

"I know all the words for 'money'," Dylan explained.

"Avalon ducats," Squire Edwin said. He started handing round the leather sacks. "The currency of our realm. I pray you spend them wisely," he said as Timmy took one in his mouth.

Dylan cradled his bag of money and inhaled its sweet aroma. "Cometh to papa!" he crooned.

"Have at you, I say!" They heard Blaine Dunston's voice somewhere off among the tents.

Following the sound, the Five spotted Blaine in full armour, sparring in a wooden sword battle with Prince Roland. Prince Roland had adopted a defensive stance and was waiting for Blaine to tire. As they watched, Blaine's visor dropped with a clang. He swung his sword more wildly than ever, veering, staggering and windmilling his arms. Eventually he got dizzy and fell to the ground. Prince Roland hadn't moved a muscle.

Blaine tried to stand up but – rather like a turtle on its back – he found that he was stuck. "There," he said, his voice muffled by the visor. "I win."

Daine Dunston and the Dunstons' servant Crawford rushed forward to help Blaine back on to his feet. All three fell over with a resounding clang.

"This is an outrage!" shrilled Daine. "Crawford, contact our lawyer immediately. It's lawsuit time!"

"His fall was worse than King Oliver's," Jo said as Prince Roland removed his helmet. "Oh, but you didn't see that, did you Prince?"

Prince Roland smiled and gestured at a nearby pavilion, where King Oliver, Princess Petula, Allie and assorted others were dancing a medieval bagatelle to the tune of a mandolin. "Alas, I was absent, helping Princess Petula with her dance steps," he explained. "But now, a passage at arms . . ." He passed his helmet to Jo. "Take this, please . . ."

"It's about time!" Jo said eagerly, seizing the helmet.

". . . and help Sir Max put it on, that he be properly armed for combat," Prince Roland continued. "You, maiden, can then amuse yourself at the dance pavilion."

Jo glared at Roland. She shoved the helmet into Max's midriff, winding him.

"Oooof," Max gasped. "It's a good thing you didn't live in the Middle Ages, Jo – I don't think you'd have fitted in."

Chapter Four

Allie was making the most of her medieval dancing opportunity. She whirled gracefully between King Oliver, Princess Petula and the several-left-footed Squire Edwin, exchanging partners over and over as the dance progressed. When she got close enough, Allie spoke eagerly to the princess.

"Tell me, Princess, how did you all come to Avalon Island?"

"King Oliver and I are betrothed in marriage and Prince Roland is his royal cousin," the princess explained, twirling past.

"Verily?" Allie said in delight. "You know – for real or pretend?"

Princess Petula glanced towards Prince Roland as he sparred with Max. "Verily indeed," she smiled.

Allie now turned towards her gangly new partner. Squire Edwin took a step backwards. His doublet got snagged on a nail in the post holding up the pavilion. As he started towards Allie to take her hand, he pulled the post, bringing the entire pavilion down on the dancers' heads.

"Ohhhhh," he moaned.

"Woaah," Allie squealed, jumping back.

"Edwin, you're an idiot," Squire Edwin said mournfully from beneath yards of billowing fabric. "Come on – focus!"

Dylan meanwhile had approached a stall selling golden crowns, chains, sceptres and rings.

"Greetings, young squire," said the old stallholder as he hitched up his craftsman's robes, "and welcome to Silas's Treasure Trove."

"Fancy trinkets, Si," Dylan said appreciatively, hunting through the stall. "But tell me this – do you have any saws? Like I might use if I wanted to, say, saw through a strut upon which someone – King Oliver, for instance – might be standing?"

Silas the stallholder shook his head. "No. Just yon

shiny trinkets," he explained. He held up a silver circlet so that it caught the sunlight. "These circlets, for instance. Much desired by all and sundry."

Dylan heard Constable Stubblefield's voice. He turned to see the police officer, in a frilly gown with a long train, pushing through the crowd.

"That's exactly what I need to win the heart of Prince Roland, who I sense is more than a little taken with me," Constable Stubblefield was saying, bearing down on the circlets with a gleam in her eye.

"How much for that?" Dylan quickly asked Silas before Constable Stubblefield reached the stall.

"Three ducats," Silas told him.

"I'll take it. I'll take everything." Dylan handed Silas his whole bag of ducats.

Constable Stubblefield had arrived at the stall. "I've *got* to have that pretty Prince Roland circlet," she demanded.

"Excellent," Dylan smiled, sidling behind the stall. "Six ducats."

Constable Stubblefield looked shocked. "They were three ducats a minute ago," she protested.

"Well, there's a three-ducat handling charge," Dylan explained. He patted the circlet. "There. I've handled it. Six ducats."

Grumbling, Stubblefield handed over her money. Dylan smiled to himself. "Time to fleece the flock . . ." he murmured. He jumped up on to the stall counter and broke into song.

"TA-RA-RA-BOOM-DE-AY," he sang, jigging vigorously, *"THERE IS A SALE TODAY: WITH EVERYTHING YOU BUY, YOU GET A FREE PORK PIE. Pork pies subject to availability . . ."*

People flocked to the stall, waving their money.

"There you go," Dylan said, taking the ducats and distributing the merchandise as quickly as he could. "Sorry, we don't have pork pies yet . . . Thank you – no pork pies right now . . . Please come again – we're trying to get pork pies, I know a man . . ."

In the feasting tent, the guests were lined up on benches spanning a long table which was piled with eat-with-your-hands food. Allie nibbled on a turkey leg, trying to be dainty, but Jo and Max were tucking in with abandon. Even Timmy had his own place at the table, with a bib around his neck and a dog dish in front of him. Jo belched and tossed her half-eaten beef rib into Timmy's dish, where Timmy happily gnawed on it.

"My hands are disgustingly greasy – yeachh," Daine complained as she finished a rib.

Dylan appeared from nowhere. "Hands greasy?" he asked, waggling his eyebrows behind his glasses. "Face a mess? Irritated by unsightly pox? You needeth me, Sir Wipes-A-Lot. Keep your hands clean day and . . .*knight.*" With a flourish, he wheeled in a suit of armour and pulled a wipe out of the helmet's visor. Another wipe appeared in the same place, like a box of tissues. "Towel, my greasy lady?" he invited, offering Daine a wipe.

Daine took the wipe. Quick as a flash, Dylan added: "That'll be five ducats."

"That's daylight robbery," Daine gasped, horrified.

"That's good business," Dylan corrected her. "I bought every towel in the place."

Daine pouted, but handed over the money. As other guests started buying towels from Dylan, Prince Roland rose and raised his goblet. The Five and all the other guests joined him in a toast.

"Gentlefolk, I propose a toast," Prince Roland declared. "Long live King Oliver!"

"Long live King Oliver!" cried the guests.

Prince Roland took a deep gulp from his goblet. Then, as rehearsed, he staggered forward, his face turning pale as he grabbed his throat. He gurgled and toppled over, dead to the world.

King Oliver leaped to his feet. "O villainy! Let the doors be locked! Prince Roland is poisoned!" he cried.

The Five were instantly alert. They exchanged

glances, already on the case.

"My subjects," said King Oliver gravely as the consternation died down. "Your quest is to discover the perpetrator behind this foul crime afore the weekend is out." His expression transformed into a big smile. "But first," he said, "some entertainment!"

A Merlin-like sorcerer began to perform various tricks, pouring flasks of chemicals together to make flashes of floating lights and explosions. The guests oohed and aahed with delight. The show concluded in an explosion of coloured smoke, which cleared to reveal that the sorcerer had disappeared.

"Great!" Max enthused, clapping hard along with everyone else. "It's really the best after-poisoning entertainment I've ever seen."

Safely away from all the feasting, a figure knelt down in King Oliver's tent to pull aside a hanging tapestry – and reveal a steel safe. His gloved hands dialled the combination and unlocked the safe to reveal piles of banknotes. It was the work of moments to stuff the notes into a chest – and disappear as silently as he had come.

Chapter Five

Back in the feasting tent, the guests were milling round with note pads and quills, questioning King Oliver, Princess Petula and the sorcerer, whose name was Leonard the Spellcaster.

"King Oliver," said Blaine as he and his sister cornered the king with their quills at the ready. "We have an utterly important question for you about the awful and tragic poisoning!"

"Yes," Daine butted in. "Do we get a reward?"

"Sweet prince!" Constable Stubblefield struck a dramatic pose as she looked at the prone Prince Roland. Princess Petula gave her a dubious look. "His love for me must have driven him to destruction at the hand of a rival," Constable Stubblefield continued. "Oh, curse the spell I cast on men." She left the tent forlornly, her long train taking out several candle stands and half the furniture.

Timmy tugged on King Oliver's robe. The king duly turned his attention to the Five.

"Listen, Your Royal What-sis," Jo began, "did you notice anyone around the ramparts before the boat got here this—"

"King Oliver!" Squire Edwin shouted, galloping into the tent and interrupting Jo's line of questioning. "King Oliver! Ooofff . . ."

He had tripped over the legs of Prince Roland, who stayed remarkably still. Clambering back on to his feet, Squire Edwin reached the king and whispered something urgent in his ear. King Oliver reacted in alarm, and rushed out of the tent. The Five raced out of the tent after him, with Squire Edwin following close behind.

King Oliver dashed into his tent. Minutes later, the Five found him there, on his knees in front of the empty safe.

"Every penny of our earnings – stolen!" the king

moaned, dropping his face into his hands. "Avalon Island is finished forever! I'll have to go back to busking on the underground."

Dylan inspected the safe, giving the dial an easy turn. "The lock wasn't forced," he concluded. "Whoever cracked this puppy knew the combination."

"Impossible!" King Oliver declared at once. "The only person I told the combination to was Squire Edwin."

The Five turned as one body towards to Squire Edwin.

"And I didn't tell a soul!" Squire Edwin protested, looking embarrassed. "Except for Leonard the Spellcaster," he amended. "And of course Cyril the Fletcher. And Minnie the Cooper needed to know. Oh, and Percy the Pig Farmer . . ."

"So," Jo said sarcastically, "the only people who knew the combination was everyone. Huh – that narrows it down."

"Please, my friends," implored King Oliver, "no word of this theft to the other guests. We mustn't ruin their enjoyment."

Allie shrugged. "Whatever thou sayest . . ."

25

Timmy sniffed at the safe and growled. Max bent down and inspected a waxy handprint on the safe door. As he studied it, the visor on his helmet clanged shut. He opened the visor, ran his finger across the handprint and then rubbed his fingers together thoughtfully. "Hmm," he said, bringing his finger up to his eyes for a closer look. The helmet obliged by slamming shut again.

"Ow!" Max shouted, shaking his finger. "This helmet needs a kickstand."

The Five left the King, Edwin and Leonard in the tent and went outside.

"Whoever stole that money is stuck here till the boat returns," Jo pointed out. "That gives us a few hours."

"You lot get on with that. I've got some jester's hats to sell," said Dylan. He paused, then brightened. "I've got it," he said triumphantly. "'You'll flip for a jester's hat'!"

To demonstrate, Dylan did a back-flip, crashing through the door of a nearby privy. "Ow," he added in a muffled voice as the door swung shut on him.

"Check out this wax," Max said, showing his hand to the others. "It was on the door of the safe.

Whoever opened it had wax on their fingers."

"Let's pay a visit to the candlemaker," Jo suggested. "Maybe he can shed some light on this . . ."

"Hee-hee," Allie chuckled in delight, "pun!"

Chapter Six

Back in Avalon village, the Five approached a figure beneath a sign bearing the mark of a candle. The candlemaker turned, to reveal a familiar face wearing a big fake nose and a pair of spectacles.

"Leonard the Spellcaster?!" Dylan said in surprise.

"Shhh!" said Leonard, adjusting his nose. "I'm Gremio the Candlemaker! We actors here at Avalon delight in playing multiple roles ... " He gestured to a few goats surrounding a grimy lady goatherd playing a pipe. "Princess Petula is also Nellie the Goat Hag."

The Five gazed at the lady as her goats butted

her into the mud, one of them even going so far as to eat her pipe.

"Prince Roland is Ned the Woodcarver," Leonard continued, as a familiar-looking craftsman in a woodcarver's hut stood up from planing some wood with a shredded apron, one sleeve left on his shirt and only half a moustache on his face to show for his pains. "And Squire Edwin . . ."

They all watched as Squire Edwin tripped over a goat and landed in a nearby watering trough with a splash.

"Well," Leonard said eventually, "he's got his hands full just being Squire Edwin." He resumed his role as Gremio the Candlemaker. "I expect you have questions as to the mystery of Prince Roland's poisoning."

Jo shook her head. "We're investigating a real crime." She inspected Leonard's hand. "Making candles must get wax all over your hands," she said casually. "The hands that stole the money from King Oliver's safe!"

"Someone stole money from the safe?" Leonard gasped, his face draining of colour. "What?!"

"Don't play dumb, Magic Man," said Dylan, stepping up to the old man. "It happened right after you disappeared in a burst of smoke."

Leonard looked around for a moment, then hurled something to the floor. There was a puff of smoke. As it cleared, the Kirrins gazed in confusion at the spot where, only moments earlier, Leonard had been standing. There was no one there.

After a second, Leonard peered out from behind a tent flap, holding his hands up. "I hide behind the tapestry in the dining tent," he explained. "That's the act." Then he pointed at his empty candle stall.

"And I haven't touched any wax since Squire Edwin took all my candles a few days ago."

"Hey!" Jo said, turning around. "Edwin!"

Looking surprised, Edwin pointed to himself questioningly. "Who, me-est?" he said. "I mean, me?"

"Give it up, Edwin," Max said. "We know you did it."

Edwin looked nervous. Throwing his trumpet down, he turned and fled. Timmy caught the trumpet in his teeth, and the Five broke into a run, chasing the fleeing squire.

"The deceased Prince Roland loved me . . ." Constable Stubblefield murmured dreamily, plucking petals from a daisy as she sat directly in Edwin's path. "The deceased Prince Roland loved me not . . . The deceased Prince Prince Roland – oooophhh . . ."

Edwin collided with the police officer, sending her daisy flying up into the air.

"He loves you," said Allie, catching the daisy deftly and thrusting it back into Constable Stubblefield's hands as she raced by. "But Prince Roland is fictional, in addition to being 'dead' – so I'd keep shopping around if I were you."

Squire Edwin had already reached the ruins near the cliffs, with Timmy and the others gaining quickly. Jo seized the trumpet out of Timmy's mouth with one hand and removed the laces from her bodice with the other. She tied the long lace to the end of the trumpet and whirled it around like a South American bolo, which she flung at Edwin's feet with deadly accuracy. Edwin tripped and went down. He started to get up, but Timmy was on him and growling fiercely.

"Oh," he mumbled, cowed by Timmy's teeth. "Maybe I'll just lie down."

He lay back down co-operatively as the rest of the Kirrins arrived. "OK, you caught me," he said. "I did it."

"Why would you rob the safe?" Jo demanded.

Squire Edwin looked horrified. "I didn't do that," he protested. "I'd never do that."

Allie frowned. "Then what *did* you do?"

Reaching behind his back, Squire Edwin guiltily pulled out a squashed pastry. "I stole this pastry," he mumbled. "I wanted dessert. Verily!"

"Why didn't you just buy it?" Max asked.

"I couldn't afford to!" Edwin said. "The price

has tripled ever since Dylan bought out the baker's shop."

Dylan raised his hands. "Hey, a medieval merchant's got to make a living. Tell you what, you can have the pastry half price."

His cousins gave him a long, hard look. Dylan shrank back, then shook his head and sighed. "One third?" he said hopefully. "Ten per cent? OK, OK, have it for free."

"One more thing," Jo said as Squire Edwin munched ravenously on his pastry. "Why did you take all of Leonard the Spellcaster's candles?"

"They were for Prince Roland," Edwin mumbled through a mouthful. "He had me buy every candle on the island." He paused mid-bite and considered. "There's lots going on this weekend that isn't in the script."

The Five shared a look.

"Why does Roland need all those candles?" Jo said. "Is he afraid of the dark?"

Just then, Timmy's nose twitched. He started to follow a scent trail that led him to a ruined well nearby. Standing with his paws up on the well, he barked at the others.

Obediently, the Five inspected the well. Allie rubbed her finger over a stone.

"These stones feel like my lavender lip balm," she said, staring at her fingers. "Waxy. Someone's been kissing these stones!"

The others looked confused.

"People kiss the Blarney stone," Allie pointed out defensively.

Jo tested the well rope crank, but it barely moved. The rope was attached to something heavy.

"I don't think that's a bucket at the end of this rope," Jo said, and started to pull.

Max helped Jo turn the well crank handle. The head and shoulders of Prince Roland popped over the lip of the well.

Timmy barked as Dylan grabbed Roland's arm, which had a bag tangled around it. "Nope," Dylan said, as if Timmy had just asked him a question, "it's Prince Roland. I wonder why . . . Aarrggh!"

The whole of Prince Roland's arm had come away in his hand.

Jo reached over and squeezed Prince Roland's nose experimentally. It squidged into a different shape, and stayed there.

"A wax dummy!" Jo said. "So this is what all those candles were used for . . ."

Dylan opened the bag tangled around the waxen Prince Roland's arm and pulled out a handsaw. "And I'm guessing this is what sawed through the rampart strut," he said, holding up the saw to show the others.

"Seems like poisoning isn't the only mystery Prince Roland's involved in," Allie said.

"Comest, kinsfolk," Max announced. He drew

his wooden sword and held it aloft. "We hast a blackguard and a villain to question! Y'know," he confided to the others in a pleased kind of voice, "it's fun talking like that."

Chapter Seven

The Five had hardly re-entered the village when Blaine and Daine Dunston raced up to Dylan.

"Dylan," Blaine said as he hopped uncomfortably from foot to foot, "I demand you sell us some privy paper immediately!"

Shrugging, Dylan reached into his tunic and pulled out a toilet roll. "The price has gone up," he said, waving the paper temptingly. "I'll swap it for your MP3 player."

"Give it to him, Blaine," Daine begged, looking even more uncomfortable than her brother. "I can't believe we have to deal with these idiotic Kirrins . . ."

"Oops – price just went up again," Dylan said. "I'm afraid I'm going to have to ask you to hop up and down and honk like geese."

"Good job, Dylan," Jo grinned as the Dunston twins bitterly started doing what they were told. "Keep raising the price – we'll go and find Roland."

Jo, Allie, Max and Timmy approached the tent by the woodcarving table, where Constable Stubblefield was lingering dreamily, strumming a harp.

"Uhm, fair maiden Stubblefield," said Allie, "we seek Prince Roland."

Constable Stubblefield nodded graciously. "As I returned from my daily weight-lifting exercises, I spied the comely man heading for the beach," she said. "I await his return to present him with this carving I've made . . ." She proudly held up a shapeless piece of wood for the Five to admire.

"Hey!" Max said, groping for something to say. "Awesome – elephant seal!"

Constable Stubblefield looked taken aback. "It's me!" she said with a frown.

Max winced. "Yeah, it's . . . Now that you . . ."

He fumbled, adding with some relief: "We've got to go to the beach!"

He, Allie, Jo and Timmy scurried away. On the way to the beach, they passed Dylan. He was still watching over the hapless Dunstons as they crawled around on their hands and knees, braying like donkeys.

Down by the sea, waves crashed on to the shore. There were hundreds of boulders that a villain like Prince Roland might hide behind.

"I'll look in that direction," Jo said as she pointed up the coast. "Yell if you see anything."

Everyone headed different ways, with Timmy eagerly sniffing the sand and waving his plumy tail.

As Max walked around a rocky outcrop, he saw Prince Roland pushing a heavy, medieval-style chest toward a beached boat.

"Excuse me," Max said, stopping dead. "I don't think that belongs to you."

Prince Roland whirled round as he heard Max's voice. He drew his wooden sword. Refusing to be cowed, Max drew his own wooden blade and faced the prince.

"Lay on, Sir Max," Prince Roland snarled.

After a couple of feints, the prince unleashed a flurry of attacks, forcing Max to defend himself. "Not bad for a beginner," Prince Roland panted as the two of them separated for a moment.

"I learn quickly," Max replied. "I've also learned you're a coward and a thief."

Prince Roland attacked Max in fury, driving him along a spit of rocks where the waves crashed over their feet. With a flick of his wrist, he disarmed Max.

"Erm, that remark about you being a coward and a thief?" said Max weakly. "Is it too late to take it back?"

With a nasty smile, Prince Roland poked Max in the chest with his sword, knocking him backwards into the water.

"WAAAGGHHH!" Max yelled, flailing his arms. It was no good. The cold water engulfed him and sucked him under.

Chapter Eight

Further down the beach, Allie turned in alarm at the sound of Max's scream. Jo also whipped round, and Timmy's ears pricked up. They raced to the rock spit, where Prince Roland stood with his back to the beach. He was looking down at Max, who was still clinging to the rocks with his fingertips as the waves buffeted him about.

"A coward, thief and finger-stomper," Prince Roland offered, and slowly placed his boot down on Max's fingers.

Max let go. He was swept out into a whirlpool off the rocks, where he had to tread water as best he could. Jo raced up to Roland and spun him round.

She picked up Max's discarded sword, and wielded it menacingly. Unable to resist the challenge, Roland raised his own sword and followed Jo down the beach.

"All right," said Allie breathlessly as she and Timmy scurried to the edge of the rock spit and saw Max swimming hard against the whirlpool. "Time for a little something I learned from Rapunzel."

She pulled off her long braided wig and tossed one of the pigtails out to Max. Max grabbed hold. Winding the other pigtail round a sturdy nearby boulder, Allie used it for leverage as she and Timmy pulled Max to safety.

"Thanks," Max said, coughing up salt water. "I like that hair style a *lot*."

"It's about time you learned how a lady fights," Jo snarled at Roland further down the beach. She twirled her sword with the deft ferocity of a ninja warrior, did an impressive flip through the air and landed right in front of him with the tip of her sword pressed against his nose.

"Oh," Prince Roland gasped, taken completely by surprise. "In that case, I'll just be going . . ."

He threw his sword at Jo, who flashed out her

arm and caught it. But before Jo could stop him, Prince Roland raced out into the water, dived into a wave and disappeared.

The Five hurried to the chest Roland had left behind on the sand. Jo opened it, to find that it was full of cash. "Well," she said after a moment of disappointment. "One fish got away, but we still caught a whopper. Let's get this back to the king . . ."

"King Oliver?" Allie gasped, as she stumbled into the king's tent with her dress torn and muddy and her wig looking a little the worse for wear. "We have good news!"

Timmy and Max followed, with Jo bringing up the rear with the chest in her arms. The tent appeared to be empty. Then Princess Petula stepped out from behind a tapestry screen.

"The King is out," said the princess, eyeing the chest with surprise. "He's negotiating with your cousin for some privy paper."

"Afff," Jo grunted as she put the chest down. "Princess Petula, Avalon Island is saved. We've found the missing money. And the culprit is—"

"Toot, toodle-ooo," Max trumpeted, using his fingers to form an imaginary trumpet valve.

"The Dark Prince Roland," Jo concluded with a flourish.

Princess Petula looked flabbergasted. She took hold of the chest.

"When he 'died' at the banquet, he wasn't as dead as he looked . . ." Allie said.

"During the feast, everyone saw Prince Roland playing dead all the time . . ." Jo launched into her explanation as everyone in the tent brought the night in question back into their minds.

"Speaking of the feast," Allie cut in, "if I could get the recipe for those turkey drumsticks, that would be great. There was some sort of spice on them."

"Rosemary," said Princess Petula, still staring at the chest.

"Oh! Rosemary!" Allie said, pleased. "OK, all right, Jo, keep re-capping . . ."

Jo resumed. "But during Leonard the Spellcaster's act, he replaced himself with a wax dummy he'd made. Then he robbed the safe, and sneaked back while everyone was looking for his poisoner. And he had the perfect alibi – he was 'dead'!"

Max held up the wax dummy's arm. "He was pretty clever," he declared. "I've got to 'hand' it to him." Chuckling, Max added: "I've been waiting to do that one."

Princess Petula closed the chest. She smiled at the Five, then started walking towards the tent exit. Timmy grabbed the hem of her gown with his teeth to stop her leaving.

"Brilliant," Princess Petula said, trying to drag her skirt from Timmy's jaws. "But you missed one thing . . ."

In an imitation of Max's earlier imaginary fanfare, the princess raised her fingers and gave a little tootle of her own.

"I didn't do it alone," said Prince Roland's voice.

Princess Petula opened the tent flap to reveal the prince standing outside the tent. She joined him and handed over the chest, still trying to pull her gown away from Timmy.

"We can't leave Avalon Island until the next boat arrives," Prince Roland declared. "Until then, we have our roles to play."

Princess Petula gave a nasty smile. "Although, *you* won't be around to see it," she said.

45

She yanked on a nearby guy rope, and the tent collapsed on Allie, Jo and Max.

"Hey . . . What the . . . Ohhhh, I can't see – oh, sorry . . ." gasped the cousins as they were plunged into darkness.

Princess Petula hitched the guy rope to the pommel of a nearby horse's saddle. Then Prince Roland clicked his tongue at the horse. The beast began to drag the tent containing the struggling Jo, Max and Allie away – down to the water's edge.

Chapter Nine

A black nose pushed its way out of a gap in the balled-up tent as it trundled over the ground. It was quickly followed by the rest of Timmy, who dashed away, racing for the centre of Avalon village.

Outside the sleeping quarters, a number of people – including Constable Stubblefield, Blaine and Daine Dunston, their servant Crawford and the rest of the guests, Leonard the Spellcaster, King Oliver and Squire Edwin – were lining up patiently. Inside the tent itself, Dylan was looking quite comfortable on a throne, a large pile of Avalon ducats on the table in front of him. Various medieval goods were stacked up in the background.

"Good merchant," Constable Stubblefield said, curtseying to Dylan as she entered the tent, "I come to buy perfume. I wish to impress the gentlemen tonight, and I smell like a badger."

She raised one arm in the air to demonstrate.

"Whoa!" said Dylan, holding his nose and hastily handing her a spray bottle. "Put your arm down and I'll cut the price in half."

Timmy raced through the tent flap and seized Dylan's arm with his teeth.

"Wahhh!" Dylan objected, falling off his throne as Timmy tugged. "OK, I'm coming, I'm coming . . ."

As Dylan departed with Timmy, Stubblefield spritzed her neck lightly with perfume, then emptied the whole bottle over herself just in case.

The jetty in Avalon harbour was deserted. Underneath its weathered boards, however, it was looking distinctly crowded. Jo, Max, and Allie were all tied to the pilings, the chest-high waves washing against them.

"Woooah!" Allie wailed, as a large wave crashed over her. As it cleared, it revealed a fresh green wig of seaweed hanging from her head.

Max laughed hysterically.

"Don't laugh," Allie complained. "I can't help it."

"I'm not laughing at you," Max roared, tears in his eyes. "There's a mackerel in my trousers – it's tickling!"

Dylan's upside-down head appeared from above the jetty.

"I'd get out of there if I were you," he said, giving them an upside-down thumbs-up and a smile. "The tide's coming in."

Back at the feasting tent, the grand finale of the Medieval Murder Mystery was reaching its climax.

Constable Stubblefield, Blaine, Daine, Crawford and the rest of the guests were tucking in to the feast at the long table when King Oliver and Princess Petula, in their usual seats at the high table, suddenly looked up in dramatic alarm. Princes Petula swooned at the king's side as Prince Roland, his face pale and blue, entered the tent, his eyes glazed and his movements slow and ghostlike.

"Prince Roland's ghost!" King Oliver cried with a dramatic gasp. "It cannot rest until this crime be solved!" He raised his hands to the assembled guests, who had stopped eating and were watching the drama with excitement. "Noble guests," the king entreated, "the time has come for your theories as to the author of this crime."

The guests murmured and mumbled among themselves. No one had a clue.

Constable Stubblefield leaped to her feet. "It was *you*, King Oliver!" she accused, pointing at the king with a shaking finger before throwing her arms around the blue Prince Roland in a crushing hug. "When you saw noble Prince Roland had fallen for me, your jealousy raged," she said, her voice muffled by Prince Roland's doublet. "You poisoned Prince Roland so you could have me for your own!"

An uncomfortable silence fell across the tent as Prince Roland tried to extract himself from Constable Stubblefield's vice-like grip.

"Hast anyone else any ideas?" asked the king hopefully.

A ghostly moan floated through the air. Max, Allie, Dylan and Timmy stepped out from behind the tapestry, while Jo emerged from behind the throne.

"Forsooth," Jo announced, "Prince Roland and

Princess Petula are the culprits."

"They were the ones who sawed through the strut on the ramparts!" Dylan said.

"They were the ones who took the money!" added Allie.

"And they were going to escape while we were conveniently drowning," Max put in. "Which is pretty rotten of them, if you think about it."

King Oliver shook his head in disbelief. "No," he said. "Petula and Roland would never do that to me."

Princess Petula looked at King Oliver briefly. Then she picked up the chest from behind her throne and joined Prince Roland. "Sorry, Ollie," she said with a shrug, "but Avalon just ain't my idea of an island paradise."

"Petula and I are getting married," Roland said. "On a real island, like Bermuda." He took the chest from Petula. "Come on, love," he said, dropping his princely accent at last. "Time for our final bow."

As King Oliver sank on to his throne with a devastated expression on his face, the lovers headed for the exit.

Constable Stubblefield suddenly came to life.

"If I can't have him, no one can!" she bellowed. And she grabbed a turkey leg from the table and lobbed it at Prince Roland.

Chapter Ten

"Owwww!" Prince Roland shouted, reeling backwards as the turkey leg caught him on the shoulder.

The Five shared a look. Then they each grabbed a turkey leg and began to hurl them at the villains. Prince Roland and Princess Petula were pelted with drumsticks from all sides. Prince Roland drew his sword as Princess Petula ducked behind a chair. Max and Jo grabbed a fresh set of turkey legs as though they were swords, then faced Prince Roland. The three began to duel.

"Let's see how you do against *two* knights!" Max shouted.

The air was filled with turkey and vegetables as

all the guests joined in the food fight. Daine and Blaine dived for cover under the table as flying food whipped past. Re-emerging with caution, they were immediately knocked over by a flying turkey leg and a cabbage.

"Woaahh!" yelled Blaine.

"Ahhhh!" squealed Daine.

Petula tried to crawl out of the tent, but came face to face with a snarling Timmy.

She retreated rapidly and grabbed a shield.

As Max, Jo and Roland battled on with their turkey legs and sword, Allie looked at the golden tresses still cascading from her head. "Who wants to be a lady, anyway?" she said at last. Removing her wig, she grabbed a nearby pumpkin and, using the wig as a sling shot, whipped it round and let the pumpkin fly. With pinpoint accuracy, the pumpkin slammed into Princess Petula's shield, and sent her staggering backwards.

"Woahhhh . . ." gasped the princess, landing in a heap as her purse spilled golden ducats on the floor.

"I'm also a fortune teller," Dylan said, leaning in to the princess as she struggled to her feet. "'You'll have a bad day today.' That'll be forty ducats, please." And he helped himself to the ducats on the floor and put them in his sack.

Max and Jo attacked Prince Roland with a co-ordinated volley of blows from their turkey legs, forcing him backwards. As Max disarmed the dark-haired villain, Jo lunged and knocked Prince Roland to the floor with her turkey leg. He landed next to Princess Petula.

Dusting off their hands in triumph, the food-spattered Five gathered round the dazed and somewhat stained Prince Roland and Princess Petula.

"Good night, sweet prince . . ." Jo said cheerfully.

Back on policing duty, Constable Stubblefield loaded a handcuffed Roland and Petula into the boat down on the jetty. The other guests loafed around, waiting to board, while Dylan sat organizing his bartered goods: a mountain of MP3 players, cellphones, watches and CDs.

"Dylan," said King Oliver jovially as he approached with the other Kirrins, "your cousins tell me you've acquired great wealth here on the island."

"I don't like to brag, but I'm just better than everyone else," Dylan said modestly. "You know how it is."

"Congratulations to you," said King Oliver. "As long as you pay the departure tax. One hundred ducats."

Dylan looked anxious. "I got rid of all my ducats," he said. "They're not worth anything off the island. Guys?" he said to the others. "Can I borrow some ducats?"

"Sorry," said Jo, "you had all of ours."

"Ah, well," said King Oliver. "I suppose your bartered goods will do."

As Dylan goggled at him, the king turned to the other guests. "Departing guests," he invited, "I bid you reclaim your booty!"

The guests swarmed over Dylan's pile of goods. Powerless to resist, Dylan looked on sadly.

"I can cheer you up," Max offered, patting Dylan on the shoulder. From behind his back, Max produced a flapping fish, which he dropped down the back of Dylan's trousers. Dylan dissolved into helpless giggles.

"Thank you, my subjects," said King Oliver, raising his hands to the Five. "Your cleverness has saved my treasury, and the realm of Avalon Island!" He drew his wooden sword and held it over the cousins. "I dub thee noble knights and ladies of Avalon forever!" he intoned.

"Huzzah!" cheered the cousins. Timmy barked with delight.

"By the way, sire," Jo said, "just who *did* 'poison' Prince Roland?"

King Oliver grinned. "Ah, it's a big surprise. It

was an 'accident'. It turns out a clumsy servant mistakenly drops rat poison into the fatal goblet."

Jo frowned. "A clumsy servant? That could only be . . ."

"*Squire Edwin!*" chorused the others.

And with a bow, Squire Edwin blew a final fanfare on his trumpet.

Epilogue

Out in the sunshine on Avalon Island, Max focused the videocamera on Allie, who was standing next to a steaming wooden tub.

"Sticky Situation Number One Thousand and Eight," Max introduced: "You Need To Make Dye."

Allie held up a piece of homespun beige fabric to the camera. "In the Middle Ages, they had to make dye from plant roots," she began. "*You* might be stuck in the middle of nowhere sometime, but you still want your clothes to look good."

Leaning down, she yanked up a nearby plant by the roots. "If you soak the roots of the plant in hot water long enough," she continued, "eventually they dye the water the colour you want. Then you can dye your clothes."

As Max tracked her with the camera, Allie carried the fabric towards the wooden tub. To her surprise, a dark purple Dylan emerged from the tub as she approached.

"This *wasn't* the hot tub, was it?" Dylan spluttered.

Allie turned back to the camera with a sweet smile. "Or," she said, "if you have a goofball like Dylan around, you can make human Easter Eggs."

"Seriously," Dylan asked, staring at his purple arms, "does this stuff come off?"

"Don't worry, it does," Allie assured him as Dylan tried to scrub out the colour. "In about a month . . ."

LOOK OUT FOR THE WHOLE SERIES!

THE CASE OF THE
MESSY MUCKED UP MASTERPIECE

Hodder
Children's
Books

A division of Hachette Children's Books

**Special thanks to Lucy Courtenay
and Artful Doodlers**

First published in Great Britain in 2008 by Hodder Children's Books

1

A Catalogue record for this book is available from the British Library

ISBN 978 0 340 95982 4

Typeset in Weiss by Avon DataSet Ltd,
Bidford on Avon, Warwickshire

Printed in Great Britain by
Clays Ltd, St Ives plc

The paper and board used in this paperback by Hodder Children's
Books are natural recyclable products made from wood grown in
sustainable forests. The manufacturing processes conform to the
environmental regulations of the country of origin.

Hodder Children's Books
a division of Hachette Children's Books
338 Euston Road, London NW1 3BH
An Hachette Livre UK Company
www.hachettelivre.co.uk

Chapter One

A vast boy-shaped shadow fell across the Falcongate Town Hall.

"PEOPLE OF FALCONGATE!" boomed Max's voice. "I COME FOR PEACE. SPECIFICALLY, FOR A PIECE OF CAKE."

Grinning, Max blew his blond fringe out of his eyes and straightened up. His shadow fell away from the scale model of the Town Hall, which sat on a table in the dark, polish-scented building of the Historical Society in Falcongate. A few paintings hung around the Historical Society's walls, and there were some documents in glass cases. A doleful-looking mannequin of an

1

eighteenth-century sailor stared glassily down at the visitors.

Dylan and Jo were holding a metre-wide framed painting against the wall for Mrs Nylander – the small, scatterbrained, eighty-year-old Historical Society chairwoman – to admire. It showed an eighteenth-century coastal fort: a small, solid stone building with a few cannon on its parapets. It was beautifully painted, if wave-lashed naval scenes were your thing.

"This is *such* an addition to the Historical Society," quavered Mrs Nylander, whose thing this clearly was. "James Westbrook's painting of the Falcongate Tollbridge."

Dylan frowned and pushed his glasses up his nose. "Um, Falcongate *Fort*, Mrs Nylander," he corrected. "It's the naval fort on the coast."

"I have so much on my mind," said Mrs Nylander, looking unperturbed by her mistake. "When I say 'tollbridge', I mean 'naval fort'." She turned to Jo. "Please thank your mother, Contessa Heliotrope of Sporking Tadwell, for lending us the painting."

Jo looked confused. "Er, my mother's name is *George*."

"Did I say 'Contessa Heliotrope of Sporking Tadwell'?" said Mrs Nylander vaguely. "I meant 'George'." She eyed the painting. "Could you move it a little to the right?"

"That depends," Dylan said. "When you say 'right', do you mean 'left'?"

"Goodness, no!" Mrs Nylander tittered. "I mean 'down'."

The fourth of the Kirrin cousins, Allie, stepped into the confusion. "Mrs Nylander," she said as she flipped her long, blond, well-brushed hair back over her shoulders. "I'm really good at interior design. Do you mind if I help?" She turned to Jo and Dylan. "Tiny bit left. Up a little— AAAGGGHHHHHHHH!"

"AAAAGGHHHHH!" Jo and Dylan yelled, startled by Allie's terrified scream. The painting flew out of their hands and headed towards a suit of armour, which – worryingly – held a sharp-looking pike.

Just in time, Max stepped in and caught the painting. He handed it back to Jo and Dylan. "PEOPLE OF FALCONGATE," he intoned, using the silly voice he'd perfected over the scale model

of the Town Hall. "I GIVE YOU BACK YOUR PAINTING. GIVE ME DOUGHNUTS FOR MY PLANET."

"Sorry I screamed," Allie said, looking sheepish. "I saw a spider on that display case."

"Since when are you afraid of spiders?" Jo demanded.

"Since I saw a movie where spiders take over the world and enslave mankind," Allie explained.

Dylan looked dreamy. "Brilliant," he said. "I want that DVD for Christmas."

Allie's eyes were fixed back on the offending spider. "AAGH!" she squealed, jumping back. "It moved! Don't enslave me!"

Jo opened the door. "Timmy, do you mind?" she asked, addressing the handsome black and tan dog at her heels.

Timmy used his tail to gently brush the spider out of the door. Order restored, Dylan hung the painting. They all stood back to admire it.

"The unveiling tomorrow will be a great day for Falcongate," Mrs Nylander beamed. And for once, she didn't sound vague at all.

* * *

That night, the Historical Society lay wreathed in shadows. The door opened very quietly, and a dark figure walked up to the painting, which was now covered by a velvet curtain. Gloved hands carefully pulled the curtain aside, to reveal the painting in the moonlight.

As one hand held the curtain, the other produced a dripping rag. It wiped the rag over the painting, which smeared into a dark and streaky blur.

Chapter Two

The following day, the Historical Society hummed with excitable, hungry guests, ready for the unveiling of the James Westbrook painting. Among them, town character Al Fresco Freddy was gobbling down the refreshments and wrapping extra food in napkins to stuff into his pockets.

The Five, plus Jo's mother George, stood near the curtained canvas, beside Mrs Nylander.

"Welcome one and all to the unveiling of the long lost painting of Fort Falcongate, donated by our beloved George Kirrin," announced Mrs Nylander. With a wave of her little hand, she gestured for George to speak.

George cleared her throat. "I was searching my attic for the key to my basement, when I found the painting," she explained to the attentive crowd. "And now, here we are, enjoying free tea cakes."

Mrs Nylander stepped up to the canvas and took a corner of the curtain. "Thanks to George's generosity, I'm pleased to present the lovely 'View Of Falcongate Fort'," she said, and pulled back the curtain.

The assembled guests gasped and stared at the painting in horror. All that was left of the image of Falcongate Fort was a blurry mess of colour.

"And when I say 'lovely'," said Mrs Nylander faintly, "I mean 'appalling, smeared monstrosity'."

Max, Jo, Dylan and Allie gathered around the painting in dismay as a fierce hubbub broke out across the room.

"Oh, well," said Dylan as George stared at the mess in consternation. "So, Aunt George, what else have you got in the attic?"

Half an hour later, the audience had left, leaving only the Kirrins and local police officer, Constable Lily Stubblefield.

"So," said Constable Stubblefield to George, getting straight down to business, "the painting belonged to you. Right. I'll have you fill out the necessary paperwork and get straight on to the case."

She reached into a satchel and produced a towering stack of papers.

"We'll start with the fifteen-dash-J-slash-three-one-three form," she said, handing George the topmost sheet.

George sighed, and began filling out the form.

"Last name first," Constable Stubblefield advised, peering over George's shoulder.

As George crumpled up the form and Constable Stubblefield handed her another, the Five examined the painting.

"Hmm, no fingerprints," Jo said with a frown. "No sign of forced entry."

"What's there to force?" Dylan said, gesturing around the room. "The door doesn't even have a lock."

"Isn't Mrs Nylander afraid someone will steal the model of the old toothpick factory, made of toothpicks?" asked Max, staring at the small, industrial model in the window. "Which reminds me," he added, reaching in and snapping a toothpick off the model, "I had a poppy-seed cake for breakfast." He stuck the toothpick in his mouth and wiggled it about. "Ahhh, that's the ticket . . ."

"No locks on the windows, either," Allie said, examining the windows. "The culprit could have—SPIDER!" she screamed. Taking off her shoe, she pounded the window sill with vicious intent. Then she studied the result of her efforts. "Wait," she said after a pause. "No, it's my pendant." She held up the pieces. "Well, it *was* my pendant," she corrected, crestfallen.

"We've got to cure that phobia, Allie," Max said, shaking his head. "I used to be afraid of clowns, but I trained myself not to be. Look . . ." He picked a pie up off the abandoned buffet table and smashed it into his face. "Ooof. See?" he mumbled through a layer of pie. "The old pie-in-the-face gag. Didn't bother me a bit. Though it was a pecan pie, so it did kind of hurt."

"In the meantime, what do we do about the painting?" Jo said, still staring at the wrecked picture.

"Sell it to me!" said a bright American voice.

They turned to see a blandly handsome man with the smarmy energy of a used-car salesman striding into the room, a smile plastered across his face.

"Hi!" he declared, shaking Dylan's hand. "Honeycutt, Bob Honeycutt."

Dylan frowned at his hand and wiped it off on his trousers. Bob Honeycutt's grip was clammy.

"I'm an American art collector," Bob Honeycutt continued, stopping in front of the painting. "From America! Ever been there? It's great! Top-notch." He pointed at the ruined James Westbrook painting.

"And that's a top-notch painting," he added.

"But it's ruined," Dylan pointed out.

"It's post-expressionist!" said Honeycutt enthusiastically. "Bold! It speaks to me. It says: 'Bob – buy me'." He produced a wad of money and waved it at the Five. "How much ya want for it?"

"Ooh," Dylan murmured, his eyes brightening, "money!"

"It's not for sale," Jo cut in. "For one thing, it's evidence in a police investigation . . ."

Everyone looked across at Constable Stubblefield, who was handing George another form off the towering stack. "Form Two," the constable was explaining. "List all acquaintances from the age of two, to the present day. With addresses and phone numbers."

". . . an investigation which could take several years," Jo concluded. She frowned back at the painting. "But before that, we're going to work out who did this . . ."

Chapter Three

Back at Jo's house, the Five gathered in George's study. Jo studied an art book, while Allie read George's old journal. Dylan meanwhile studied the painting, which was now sitting on an easel.

"All of these smears go from left to right, starting from the bottom," Dylan said, pointing to the smears on the canvas. "I'll bet the culprit was left-handed."

"Well, that narrows it down to about four hundred and seventy million people," said Jo dryly, looking up from her art book. "We'd better start questioning them."

"Aunt George's old journal has some great

sketches of Falcongate Fort," said Allie, engrossed in the small, handwritten book. She shuddered. "I bet that place is crawling with spiders."

"That's it, Allie – time to cure your fear of spiders," Max announced. "I'm going to get you used to 'cute' spiders. For instance . . ." He turned his hand into a spider, and started crawling it along the desk towards his cousin. "See?" he said in a cutesy voice. "I'm Spidey, the happy spider! I'll make friends with . . ."

"AAAAGGGGH!" Allie screamed, noticing the 'spider' and slamming the journal down on Max's hand.

"Owww!" Max cradled his limp hand. "OK," he conceded, "we'll have to get some *cuter* spiders."

"Why would someone vandalize the painting?" Jo murmured, still deep inside her art book. "This book says Westbrook didn't have any enemies. Though he did owe a lot of people money."

"That reminds me, Dylan," Max said. "You owe me five pounds."

"Give me five pounds," said Dylan promptly. "I'll pay you back."

"OK," said Max, sounding pleased. "Here you go."

He pulled five pounds out of his pocket and gave it to Dylan. Dylan handed it straight back.

"There," Dylan said. "We're even."

"All right, then," Max agreed. The smile slipped off his face and a suspicious look took its place. "Wait a minute – was I just tricked?"

Dylan shrugged. "No."

Max's face cleared. "All right, then."

"Westbrook did lots of paintings of Falcongate, but except for this one, they got destroyed in a fire," Jo told the others.

Timmy raised his head. No sooner had he started barking than they all heard a knocking at the front door.

A man about fifty years old – with bushy eyebrows, mutton-chop whiskers and a moustache – stood on the front porch as the Five opened the door.

"Hello," said the individual. "I'm Wilberforce Squatney, of Lungford and Lingford Insurers." He reached out to shake Max's hand. Max wiped his palm down his trousers. The man had clammy hands.

"Sorry," Jo apologised, seizing Timmy's collar as

he continued to growl at Wilberforce Squatney. "He doesn't like strangers."

"Nor should he," agreed Wilberforce Squatney. "Bite them, is what I'd do. Lesson learned. Now, about this painting . . ."

"What, Aunt George's painting?" Allie said, heading back into the house.

"I'm given to understand it's become messy and out of sorts," said Wilberforce Squatney.

"It was vandalized," Dylan explained.

"Ra-ther," said Squatney. "My company insures it. I'm to take it to our appraisers, who will issue payment."

Allie arrived back at the door, holding the painting. She handed it to Squatney.

"Top-hole," said Wilberforce Squatney. He handed Jo a receipt. "Receipt for merchandise transferred. I bid you good-day."

He trotted off up the drive. The Five turned back and headed for the kitchen, where George was unpacking some shopping.

"Hi Mum," said Jo. "The insurance man picked up the painting."

"What insurance man?" George asked.

"Didn't you insure the painting?" said Dylan.

George shook her head. "No. Until last week, I didn't even know I *had* the painting."

"Oh boy," Dylan groaned as the Five exchanged looks. "This time, we've *all* been tricked."

Timmy stood up at the window, barking. The kids ran over to the window, to see Squatney approaching a motorcycle with a sidecar which stood parked at the foot of the drive. He quickly placed the painting into the sidecar and mounted the motorcycle.

Without a word, the Five raced from the kitchen, hopped on their bikes and took off across George's lawn, in hot pursuit of Wilberforce Squatney.

Chapter Four

As Wilberforce Squatney sped down the country lane on his motorcycle, the Five swerved in front of him, racing out of the woods that lined the road. Squatney turned sharply, veering into a farm field lined with long rows of haystacks. Crashing straight through the first haystack, he then headed for a gap between two more. Like genies popping from bottles, Dylan and Jo appeared on their bikes in the gap, blocking his way. Cursing, Squatney turned again and headed along a row of haystacks, with Dylan and Jo close on his heels.

Further up the field, Max and Allie wheeled a big tractor tyre into the fraudulent insurance man's

path. Squatney made another hard turn, heading up a different alley of haystacks. But this way was barred too, as Timmy had rolled a barrel neatly into Squatney's path.

The next obstacle was a hay wagon, which Jo and Dylan positioned at the end of the alley to keep Squatney turning, forcing him to head towards the barn in the centre of the field. Faced with no choice, Squatney sped into the barn, making for the far door. But before he could emerge, Max and Allie leaped into action, struggling to slide the heavy barn door closed. The door started swinging shut as Squatney raced towards it. In the nick of time, Squatney squeezed through the gap – but the sidecar containing the painting sheared off against the edge of the door and stayed in the barn.

Dylan and Jo rushed in to join Max and Allie.

"He got away!" Dylan cried in disappointment.

"But without the painting," Jo smiled, picking it up.

Back in George's study, the painting was on its easel once again – as if it had never been snatched in the first place.

"Why do so many people want to get their hands on this?" Jo said, frowning at the painting as Dylan paced around behind the canvas, examining the back.

"Maybe there's gold or jewels or something hidden in the frame," Dylan said, tugging at the back of the picture. "Come on, gold! Come on, jewels!" The picture toppled off the easel, landing on top of Dylan. "Ooff," he grunted. "I'll settle for silver?"

Allie was sitting at George's desk. Several antique car mascots lined the desktop, along with a container of brass polish and a rag. Max approached her.

"Spider," he whispered experimentally. Then, as Allie didn't react, he added with some relief: "Good. You didn't jump. And you didn't clobber me with . . . what are those things?"

"Uncle Ravi's old car mascots," Allie explained, soaking the rag with polish. "I told him I'd polish them."

Max whipped out a picture of a grinning cartoon spider. "What about that?" he said, jigging the picture in front of his cousin. "Is that scary?"

"Nope," said Allie. She picked up a mascot.

"See? It's working," Max said, pleased. "Cute spiders don't bother you. What about this?" He pulled out a picture of a real spider.

Allie shuddered. "Kinda ugly, but I'm good."

"How about *this*?" Max opened the door and let Timmy into the study. Timmy blinked up at Allie from beneath the spider costume Max had kitted him out in.

"That's just the cutest thing in the whole world," Allie said, her gaze softening. "Maybe I'm not really

afraid of— SPIDER!!" she shrieked, pointing at a spider crawling on the picture frame as Dylan set it back on to the easel. She hurled her polish cloth. Dylan ducked just in time, and the cloth whacked into the top of the painting, sliding down and removing another swathe of paint.

"Allie – look what you've done!" Jo gasped.

"I panicked," Allie stammered. "I'm sorry."

"Don't be sorry," Jo said, picking up the rag. "You found something!" She started scrubbing at the painting, clearing away more paint. The faint outline of a map peeped at her. It was the floor plan of a building.

"There's some sort of a map under the painting. A secret map!" Jo announced in delight.

"I'd rather have gold," Dylan muttered as the others clustered around Jo and the painting. "Hey!" he added, as Jo threw the rag at him.

Chapter Five

It took a matter of minutes to scrub away the rest of the paint. The Five studied the map which lay beneath. It showed a hexagonal floor plan, divided into many rooms with lots of connecting passageways, and there was a small round compass in the lower corner. The 'N' at the top of the compass was encased in a decorative star. A dotted line showed a route through the maze-like plan, to a room marked with an 'X'.

"The question is, what's it a map of?" Jo asked.

Max scratched his head. "Are we sure it's a map?" he asked. "It looks like a maze from the Fun Page of the newspaper."

"Why would someone put a Fun Page maze underneath a painting?" Dylan asked.

"When you tired of looking at the painting, you'd have a game to play?" Max suggested.

"Well, it's under a painting of Falcongate Fort," Allie pointed out. "And look at Aunt George's journal . . . " She reached out to pick up the journal, casually blowing off the small paper spiders that Max had cunningly placed there.

"Hey, great!" Max declared. "You're not scared of spiders any more!"

"I'm not scared of *paper* spiders," Allie said scornfully. "I'm scared of spiders that can bite me." She held up the journal. "Aunt George has a drawing of Falcongate Fort seen from above."

The little book displayed an engraving of the fort. Like the painting, it too was hexagonal.

"Maybe it *is* a map," Max conceded. He picked up the picture in its frame and struggled briefly with it. "How come maps are always so hard to fold?" he complained.

"Allie, help Max hold the map straight," Dylan said. "Can I borrow your phone?"

Allie handed him her phone, then took one end

of the frame to hold it steady.

"I think a photo might be a little easier to carry around," Dylan explained. He aimed the phone at the map.

"WAIT! STOP!" Allie shouted. She whipped out her compact and checked her hair and make-up. "OK, go ahead," she instructed, smiling brightly for the photograph.

Five minutes later, the Five left the house and mounted their bikes. From the shadow of the woods around George's property, Wilberforce Squatney sat astride his motorcycle and watched them go.

It was a short ride to Falcongate Fort, a crumbling stone structure on the coast.

"I suppose this is what happens when you don't keep up the maintenance," Dylan commented, bringing his bike to a halt near the fort's half-ruined entrance.

"In LA, they'd call this a 'fixer-upper'," Allie said. "A little landscaping, fresh coat of paint, and bang – three-point-two million dollars."

Jo shaded her eyes and stared at the fort. It didn't

look like much. "I've never been here, because I thought a bunch of crumbling rocks would be dull," she said. "How right I was."

A matronly woman was waiting for them at the main gate. According to the name badge on her uniform, she went by the unfortunate name of Lorelei Crump.

"Welcome to Fort Falcongate," Lorelei Crump said in a business-like drone. "No food, no drinks, no flash photography, no loud talking, no bare feet. Enjoy your visit."

"How?" Dylan enquired, looking perplexed.

"And no pets," Lorelei Crump added.

"Can I tie my dog up outside?" Jo asked.

Crump inclined her head briefly. "You can tether your dog *out*side. He's just not allowed *in*side."

Timmy growled softly as Jo attached his lead.

"No growling."

The list of rules appeared endless. Looking irked, Jo wordlessly handed Timmy's lead to Lorelei Crump. As she did so, her hand brushed against the woman's palm. It was clammy to the touch.

Once they were inside the fort, the kids climbed

some stone steps to a parapet, so they could look down on the semi-ruined walls of the fort's interior. Allie held up her phone, and they compared the photo of the map to the layout of walls below them.

"These walls don't match the map at all," Jo said in disappointment.

"Maybe they re-modelled," Allie suggested, glancing around. "Open up the floor plan, create some common space . . ." She pointed. "That area there would make a *great* media room."

"That area there is where they flogged pirates," Dylan informed Allie.

Allie frowned. "Waste of good natural light," she sighed.

"So it's not a map of the fort," Max concluded. "Anyone want to re-visit the Fun Page idea?"

A few minutes later, the kids emerged from the fort's main gate, looking stumped.

"I guess we could check surveyors' records at . . ." Jo stopped and looked around. "Er, where's Timmy?"

"And where's that Crump lady?" Allie added.

"I don't think that Crump lady was a lady," Dylan said suddenly. "Look . . ."

A wig, some ladies' shoes and Lorelei Crump's

uniform lay near the castle gate. Dylan put the wig on. "It was a disguise," he said, peering out from beneath the wig.

"Dylan! You're enchanting!" Max gasped, pretending to clutch at his heart.

"Do you think 'Crump' took Timmy?" Allie asked in concern as Dylan took off the wig.

"I should've known 'Crump' was phony when I felt her clammy hands," said Jo angrily.

Dylan looked alert. "Clammy?" he said. "Like putting your hand into a bowl of refrigerated slugs?"

"Hey – that insurance guy had hands just like that," said Max.

Dylan looked excited. "So did: 'Honeycutt, Bob Honeycutt, the American art collector from America'," he mimicked.

Jo picked up the wig and twirled it on her fingers. "*They* both wanted the painting," she said "What did '*she*' want?"

"The painting," Allie said. She pulled a note out of one of Lorelei Crump's shoes and handed it to Jo.

"*I've got your dog,*" Jo read. "*You've got my painting. Meet me at the old Pennington Cement Works at three-thirty.*"

"I can't *believe* he kidnapped Timmy," said Allie,

looking upset.

Max sighed. "I hope Constable Stubblefield has finally finished her paperwork."

Over at the Falcongate police station, George was still signing forms.

"There," said Constable Stubblefield soothingly, "that's the last one." She examined the form. Then she frowned. "Wait a tick – these are last year's forms! We'll have to start all over . . ."

George sighed as Stubblefield dumped another stack of papers in front of her.

Chapter Six

Down at the old Pennington Cement Works, the Kirrins made their way past a host of signs all indicating, in an assortment of languages, just how dangerous any unauthorised entry would be. Disregarding them all, they entered the cement works and found themselves amid mountains of sand and gravel that towered around them. There was a long chute leading to a loading bay, and a bucket elevator for moving sand up to the mixing point of the cement works. Timmy was in a bucket on the elevator. He barked with delight at the sight of Jo.

"Timmy!" Jo cried. "C'mere, boy!"

Timmy tried, but it was clear that he was tied up in the bucket.

"I'm afraid the pooch is all tied up," said a plummy voice behind them. "I'll release him as soon as I have the painting."

A man stepped out of the shadows. He bore a striking resemblance to the art collector Bob Honeycutt, but introduced himself as Brandon DeFunk.

"You mean 'the map', don't you?" Max said.

Brandon DeFunk's eyes narrowed. "So you found the map under the painting. I guessed you had when you went to the fort."

"If you think that's a map of the fort, you're out of luck," Allie said defiantly.

"You're also out of luck if you think you make an attractive woman," Dylan added. "Your hands are like mutton-shanks."

"It's a map of the fort, all right," DeFunk said with a smirk. "You just have to know how to read it. Now, put the painting down there and step back."

Jo set the painting down on the ground. The kids took a few paces back as DeFunk moved forward and picked it up.

"Enjoy your ride, Timmy," DeFunk laughed. He switched on the bucket elevator and disappeared back into the shadows, as the bucket containing Timmy rose up the lift shaft.

Timmy whined with surprise. Jo raced over to the elevator and started scrambling up the buckets, trying to reach Timmy. Meanwhile, the others chased DeFunk among the piles of gravel. DeFunk hopped into a little train truck and rode down to

the bottom of a gravel pit. Max, Allie and Dylan seized a wooden cargo pallet each and rode them like toboggans to the bottom of the pit – apart from Max, who rode his pallet like a surfboard with a huge grin plastered across his face.

"Wheyyyyyyy!" Max yelled with delight.

Jo seized Timmy's bucket near the top of the elevator as DeFunk scrambled up a ladder on the far side of the gravel pit, pulling the ladder up behind him. Undeterred, Max found a rope in the bottom of the pit, fashioned a lasso and threw it over a fence post up at the top. He, Dylan and Allie then used the rope to pull themselves back up to ground level.

The bucket elevator was still moving. Jo managed to untie Timmy just as their bucket overturned at the top of the elevator, and they both fell into the long, twisty, metal chute.

Still being chased by Max, Allie and Dylan, DeFunk ran past a huge pile of powdered cement. Spotting a large fan nearby, he turned it on and blew a cloud of cement at the kids. By the time they had coughed and spluttered their way into the clear, DeFunk was on his motorcycle and roaring away into the distance.

"Oooph," Jo grunted, as she and Timmy hurtled down the chute and were safely dumped into a big pile of sand at the bottom.

"Owrr," Timmy agreed.

"Good news, Jo," Max panted, skidding to a halt beside the sand pile along with Dylan and Allie. "He got away."

Jo dusted herself down. "Did he notice we gave him a fake map?" she checked.

"He was too busy running away," Allie explained.

"And we've still got the real one," Dylan said in satisfaction, unfolding the map and holding it up to the others. It displayed a large 'X' in a chamber in the south-west corner – unlike DeFunk's, which boasted an 'X' in the north-eastern corner instead.

That night, the moon shone down on Falcongate Fort, casting eerie shadows on the ground. DeFunk stood at the castle gate, studying his version of the map. After a moment's hesitation, he strode into the fort.

The Five emerged from some nearby bushes.

"All right," Jo said. "Now we'll see if he knows how to 'read the map'."

Quietly, they entered the fort. Up ahead, DeFunk was hurrying along a stone corridor. The Five silently scurried after him as he turned a corner, reaching the same corner in time to see De Funk enter a room. They tiptoed along to the doorway and peeked into the room, their heads looking as if someone had deliberately stacked them on top of each other. But all they saw was moonlight.

"Wow," said Dylan, exchanging perplexed looks with the others. "Now he's disguised himself as an empty room. He's very good . . ."

Chapter Eight

The Five gazed around the empty chamber in disappointment.

"He *can't* have just disappeared," Jo insisted.

"Care to join me in believing in aliens with tractor-beams?" Max offered. "Answers a lot of questions . . ."

They slowly sat down to ponder the mystery of the disappearing villain.

"Anyone want some water?" Allie asked, producing a sports bottle and taking a swig before offering it to the others.

Jo took the bottle and had a long drink.

"Are we sure this is the room he went into?" Allie

checked.

Dylan nodded. "Just as sure as there's a black jelly baby next to your foot," he said. Then he paused and looked more closely. "Oh, it's not a jelly baby," he amended. "It's a spider."

Allie leaped to her feet and screamed with fear. "Ew-ew-ew-ew-ew-ew-ew-ew!" she shrieked, doing a little spider dance on the spot.

Startled, Jo dropped the sports bottle. Water poured out and emptied between cracks in the stone floor.

"Allie, could you panic more quietly?" Jo pleaded as the room echoed with Allie's screams. "We don't want DeFunk to hear us."

Allie abruptly stopped shrieking, although her mouth stayed wide open and she continued dancing around. As Dylan looked at Allie in amusement, Max studied the spilled water.

"This water isn't pooling up," he said. "It's draining through the cracks."

Jo looked at the ground. "So either that's one thirsty floor, or there are other rooms underneath us," she said, back on alert.

"So maybe the map is for one of those rooms,"

Dylan concluded. "That's why it didn't match this floor plan."

"And DeFunk said if you knew how to read the map, it made sense," Max added. "I guess he knew how to get underground."

As Dylan, Jo and Max studied the map again, Allie broke into a set of fresh screams. "Ew-ew-ew-ew-ew-ew!"

Max glanced up. "Allie, remember your breathing exercises," he advised.

"Right," Allie panted, struggling to bring herself back under control. "I'm going to step outside a moment, and stop being crazy."

She stepped out of the door. A moment later, she returned. But as she re-entered the round chamber, she stopped, struck by something.

"Wow!" she squealed. "Wow-wow-wow-wow!"

"How's that not-being-crazy coming along?" Dylan enquired.

"Look at that star!" Allie cried. She pointed to a decorative star etched into a stone high on the wall of the room. "Aunt George drew that star in her journal! And look at the map . . ."

Allie pointed at the compass in the corner of the

map, indicating the decorative star encasing the 'N'. It matched the star on the wall.

"I always wanted to be a star fast bowler," Max murmured, picking up a chunk of stone broken from the wall. He hurled the stone, cricket-style, and it smashed neatly into the star on the wall. At once, a secret door pivoted open in the chamber wall, revealing stairs which led down into murky depths.

Eagerly back on the case, the cousins turned on their torches and started down the steps. The torchlight illuminated soft curtains of spiders' webs on all sides, complete with dozens of eight-legged residents.

"Aaaagghh!" Allie clapped her hand over her mouth, before adding hysterically: "I'm going outside to breathe."

"It's only a few spiders," Jo called after her as Allie ran back up the steps to the chamber, "but . . . enjoy breathing!"

Chapter Nine

The sound of Allie's running feet faded. After a moment the others walked on, and now they came to a long, underground corridor.

"Hey," Max said, looking up. "There's something dripping on me."

They shone their torches at the ceiling, where they saw old, rusty pipes running the length of the corridor. Water was dripping from them.

"Must be the old water supply for the fort," Dylan guessed. "Probably comes from out of a river near here."

"The fake map we gave DeFunk sent him to the other end of these corridors, but we still have to

hurry," said Jo, keen to chivvy the others onwards.

They rounded a corner into a small passageway, which ended in a short flight of stairs down to a heavy wooden door with a small, barred slot in it at eye level. Just before the stairs, the Five saw another door set into the corridor wall.

"If our map *is* right, this is it," Jo said in excitement.

They pushed the door open – and stared at a room full of framed paintings.

"Our map is right!" said Dylan jubilantly.

"These are all by James Westbrook!" Jo said as they moved around the room, examining the pictures.

"No pictures of dogs playing poker, or Elvis on black velvet," said Max, sounding a little regretful, "but I bet they're pretty valuable."

"They're *very* valuable," DeFunk agreed, stepping out of the shadows in the room with a stout iron bar in his hands. "And I've worked very hard to find them, so I'd appreciate it if you'd step away."

He motioned for them to move out of the room and back into the passage. As they came past him, he snatched their map away and examined it. "You

gave me an altered version of the real map," he murmured. "Clever. Awfully decent of you to have your torches on, so I could spot you."

He slowly advanced towards the cousins, smacking the bar nastily into the palm of his hand.

"How did you know the map would lead you to these paintings?" Jo asked as they backed away.

"An old letter of Westbrook's I found at an auction," DeFunk said. "In it he told his children he faked the fire that 'destroyed' his paintings."

"And he hid them down here and made a map which he covered with a painting of the fort," Dylan guessed.

They were still moving backwards, away from DeFunk and his iron bar.

"I traced the painting to your Historical Society, and you know what's happened since then," said DeFunk with a laugh.

"We do," Max said angrily. "And I still have loose gravel down my trousers, thank you very much."

They had reached the top of the short flight of stairs.

"And since I can't have you kids ruining my plan . . ." DeFunk murmured. He reached out with

41

his foot and pushed Timmy into the kids, who overbalanced and fell backwards down the steps.

"Woaahhhhh . . ." "Oww-oww-oww-oww-oww-oww-Oohhh . . ."

They clunked and clattered downwards, finally rolling through the doorway into a small stone room with no windows. DeFunk slammed the heavy, barred door shut, dislodging the water pipe fastened to the ceiling of the room. Water began gushing out of the pipe.

"Hey!" "Watch out . . ." "Ohhhh . . ." Jo, Max and Dylan scrambled out of the way as the water streamed around their feet. It was already starting to fill the chamber.

"Hey, I've already had a bath this morning," Dylan said, sounding indignant as they searched for a way out.

The water was already up to their knees.

"Who here can hold their breath for a month?" Max asked. "Show of hands . . . ?"

No one moved.

"Then let's hope Falcongate Fort has become a *really* popular tourist destination . . ." Max sighed. He scrabbled around in the water and found a hunk

of rock. Then he reached up to the pipe and began banging on it: *tap-tap-tap, tap . . . tap . . . tap, tap-tap-tap*.

Allie was still pacing around outside the fort, trying to work up the nerve to follow the others through the spider-filled corridor. "C'mon, Allie," she told herself fiercely, "it's silly to be afraid. Think of *cute* spiders, like Max said. Like the itsy-bitsy spider." Taking a deep breath, Allie started singing cheerfully: *"The itsy-bitsy spider went up the water spout, down came the—"*

As she paced, she passed near a metal pipe that stuck out of the ground and ran up the side of the fort. She heard it making a funny pinging noise.

Tap-tap-tap, tap . . . tap . . . tap . . .

"OK . . ." Allie said, pausing as she listened. *"Morse code* came up the water spout . . ."

Chapter Ten

Allie raced into the fort, heading straight for the round chamber with its hidden entrance. She sped down the steps and arrived at the beginning of the underground corridor.

The foot of the steps was crawling with spiders. Several of them were busily spinning webs up to the ceiling.

"Aw, stink," Allie moaned. She steeled herself. "OK, so it's dozens of itsy-bitsy spiders. Cute, happy little— YAAAAAAAAAA!"

She rushed wildly at the spiders, charging through the webs and down the corridor. Rounding a corner into a second corridor, she stopped to

catch her breath and wipe the webs off herself. As she glanced down the passageway, she noticed a room with its door slightly ajar. But then she heard the tapping noise again and her attention was drawn to the stout wooden door at the bottom of the steps. Water was seeping out from under it. She hurried to the leaking door, and shouted up at the small opening at the top.

"Guys?" she called. "Are you in there?"

"Allie!" Jo cried as the water level continued to rise steadily around them. "It's full of water in here. Get us out!"

"Or hand us a very long snorkel," Dylan spluttered, treading water beside Max and Timmy.

"Don't worry," Allie soothed, "I'm here."

"Yes, and that's quite inconvenient," said an irritated voice. Allie swung around to see DeFunk holding a painting and his iron bar.

"I forgot about you, Yank," said DeFunk. "It was awfully decent of you to turn yourself in."

"Well, I guess you win," said Allie, trying to sound sincere. "Should I go in there with my cousins?"

DeFunk gave a shark-like smile. "I think that would be best."

"Umm," said Allie as she lifted the latch. "Me, too . . ."

She heaved at the door and quickly stepped back behind it, to the side of the corridor.

A wave of water swept out of the chamber. It knocked DeFunk off his feet and carried him along the corridor, where he slammed backwards into the wall at the end.

"Woooaaahhh – oof – ohhhhhh," DeFunk groaned, then slumped senseless to the ground.

Max, Dylan and Jo emerged from the chamber, dripping wet. As DeFunk started to stir, Timmy raced up and stood growling over him.

"I wouldn't move," Jo advised as DeFunk opened a bleary eye and gazed at them. "Timmy's always in a very bad mood after he has a bath."

DeFunk sighed in defeat, and slumped back down in surrender.

Down at the Falcongate police station, DeFunk was clapped straight into the cell. With the Kirrins and Stubblefield gathered around, old Mrs Nylander from the Historical Society scrutinized him through the bars.

"Well, Mrs Nylander, can you identify this man?" Constable Stubblefield asked, her notebook poised and ready.

"Certainly," said Mrs Nylander at once. "That's Bob Rubberduck."

"And by 'Rubberduck', she means 'Honeycutt, Bob Honeycutt'," Dylan put in quickly.

Mrs Nylander nodded. "Exactly."

"Very well, then," said Constable Stubblefield. "Let's get started on the paperwork . . ."

She thumped a mountain of forms on to a stool in front of the cell and summoned DeFunk. "All right, you," she ordered. "Get cracking on Form one-eighteen-stroke-JSP-stroke-fifteen-A, subsections twenty-one, twenty-two, twenty-three . . ."

The cousins stepped away from the cell with Mrs Nylander, leading her to several paintings stacked against the police-station wall.

"We thought the Historical Society should have the paintings, Mrs Nylander," said Jo.

Mrs Nylander looked flabbergasted. "Goodness," she said, her hand fluttering to her chest. "Thank you ever so much, children."

The kids grinned at each other, pleased and proud.

"Our pleasure," Jo smiled.

"And when we say 'our pleasure'," Allie said with a twinkle in her eye, "we mean . . ."

"Race you to the beach!" the cousins roared at each other. "Yayyyyyyyyyyyyy . . ."

And they burst out of the station, hopped on their bikes and zoomed down to the sparkling sea.

Epilogue

The following day, Allie carefully angled the video-camera at Jo and Dylan at the kitchen table. An assortment of ingredients was laid out before them.

"Sticky Situation Number Two Hundred and Four," said Allie, adjusting the microphone. "You Have To Make Paint."

Jo looked straight into the camera. "Mix a teaspoon of cornstarch with cold water to make a paste," she announced.

Dutifully, Dylan stirred the paste in a bowl on the table.

"Then add warm water till you get the right consistency," Jo continued, watching as Dylan

49

poured in a little water from the kettle and stirred. "Then add blue food colouring, and you have blue paint."

"Which you can use to make up as William Wallace at the Battle Of Stirling Bridge," Dylan said cheerfully.

Allie panned the camera across the room, focusing on Max as he rubbed blue paint all over himself. With his hair on end and the wild look in his eye, Max looked like something from Braveheart.

"YAAAAAGGGHHHHHHHH!" Max yelled. He seized the wooden spoon that Dylan was offering him and brandished it in the air.

"Oh my goodness!" Ravi screeched, dropping the armful of groceries he was bringing in from the car.

"But it's best to warn your family first," Jo concluded a little sheepishly.

THE CASE OF THE GUY WHO
MAKES YOU ACT LIKE A CHICKEN

Read on for the
start of the Famous 5's next
Case File . . .

*Hodder
Children's
Books*

A division of Hachette Children's Books

Chapter One

It was a bright and breezy day on the crazy golf course outside Falcongate. The four Kirrin cousins (plus Jo's dog Timmy) walked towards the first hole, known as the fairy castle, cheerfully swinging their golf clubs.

"I like crazy golf," Dylan told the others as he pushed his glasses up his nose. "But it starts to get a little repetitive after the first few thousand times."

Dylan's blond-haired cousin Max jabbed the air with his finger. "That's why I've invented – speed golf!" he said. "We *run* through the course and hit the ball as fast as we can." He demonstrated. "THWACK!"

Allie pushed back her long blond hair and pointed at her shoes. "I can't run in these heels," she complained. "They pinch. Ow!"

"So do I," said Jo cheerfully as Allie rubbed her arm. She blew her dark brown fringe out of her eyes. "Speed golf sounds fun . . . but let's make it more interesting. If I win, you lot pay for my ticket to the circus tomorrow."

"So . . ." Dylan said, working it out, "if you win, I pay for you. But if I win, you pay for . . ." His brow cleared as he realized he could get to the circus for free. "GO!" he shouted, and walloped his ball.

Allie whacked her ball too, grunting with the effort. The others grabbed their putters and thumped their golf balls as hard as they could.

DOIIINNNGG! A ball ricocheted off the fairy castle. K-DINK! K-DOINK! Two balls smacked together in the air and flew in opposite directions.

The see-saw hole was next. A ball rolled on to the bottom seat and settled there. Dylan leaped on to the top seat, turning the see-saw into a catapult and hurling the ball through the air.

Balls were still flying. D-DWANG! One knocked

off a grinning leprechaun's hat. CH-CHOING! Another sent a box of golf balls flying off a shelf near the snack bar. Dozens of balls bounced everywhere.

The kids raced on round the course. A ball crashed into a ceramic fish fountain, sending the fish spinning and soaking them. Timmy the dog threw himself down just in time to duck a whizzing ball, then arched his back up as another flew under his tummy.

Jo belted her ball so hard that it bounced off both the merry-go-round hole and the Jack-in-the-box hole. Speeding on, the ball was now heading straight towards the snack bar window.

"Constantine!" Jo yelled, waving her arms. "Duck!"

Constantine, the snack bar owner, peered out of the window. "Constantine not serve duck," he said in his heavy East European accent. "Constantine serve chicken wings." His eyes widened at the sight of the ball. "Oh . . ." he said, and keeled over as it bashed him on the forehead.

The Five rushed into the snack bar. Constantine was struggling to his feet. "Constantine is fine," he said, waving his hands. "Better that ball hit

Constantine, than hit Constantine's new amazing doughnut machine."

He patted the gleaming apparatus standing next to him. "This is state of art," he said fondly. "Will make twister doughnuts such as free world has never seen."

The cousins gazed at the machine. It gleamed so much it hurt their eyes.

"There's a man who really likes his doughnut machine," said Dylan in admiration.

"Not 'like'," Constantine corrected, kissing the doughnut machine tenderly. "Love. More than family member."

But Constantine's love was not enough. The following morning, he arrived at the snack bar to find an empty spot where the new machine had been.

"Ohh," Constantine wailed, dropping to his knees. "Doughnut machine is stolen! NO-O-O-O-O! . . ."

Chapter Two

The Falcongate Victorian-style funfair and circus was in full swing. Scattered across the field were a number of small show-tents, food stalls and carnival rides. Two traditional caravans stood parked almost end-to-end, marking the entrance.

Inside the circus, the Kirrin cousins were watching a juggler. He was tossing a banana, a pineapple, a watermelon and a bowl of cherries high into the air and, somehow, catching them again.

"I don't know why," Max said, his eyes fixed on the juggler, "but suddenly I'm hungry for fruit salad."

Moving on, the cousins walked towards a showman demonstrating a contraption that

looked like a large steam-iron.

"Behold the Morning Wonder!" bellowed the showman. "Handles all your morning tasks. As you iron your shirt . . ." he demonstrated, passing the contraption over an ironing board, while a piece of toast popped out of a slot in the top end of the iron: ". . . it toasts your bread and brews your tea!" Tossing the toast to Timmy, he opened the top of the iron and poured out some tea for Jo. "And after it's made your breakfast," he continued, "it curls your hair!" With a final flourish, he pulled a curling iron out of the bottom end of the contraption.

"I'm sold," said Allie.

"Wow," Max gasped. "If that thingamabob did your homework too, it would be the greatest thingamabob in the history of thingamabobs."

Dylan was watching the showman collect money from his customers. Respect was written all over his face. "Look at all that cash!" he said to Jo and Allie. "I've got to come up with my own gadget to sell. All right, Dylan – thinking mode!"

He scrunched up his face in concentration.

"Looks more like ate-bad-oysters mode," Allie said cheerfully.

"While Dylan's off in a money trance," said Jo as they watched Dylan wander away, lost in thought, "I say we go see . . ." She waggled her fingers in Allie's face. ". . . the hypnotist. Woooo . . ."

They made their way to the hypnotist's tent and pushed their way inside. The tent was packed.

Up on the stage, a man named Harry Humpston with slicked-back hair and a goatee beard was pacing the stage. His intense eyes were locked in a gaze with Falcongate's grim twins, Blaine and Daine Dunston.

"At the sight of the queen of diamonds, you'll be in my-y-y-y-y command," said Harry Humpston in a monotone. "Voila!" He whipped out a playing card. Blaine and Daine snapped into a vacant-eyed trance.

"Blaine, you are a dog," Humpston commanded.

"Woof! Woof!" Blaine barked obediently, scratching his ear. Timmy was not impressed.

"And Daine," Harry Humpston continued, "you my dear, are a pussycat."

"Meow . . ." Daine started grooming herself, before coughing up a surprising hairball.

"And now you're locked in the same room!"

Harry Humpston told them.

Blaine began barking wildly. His sister spat and clawed at him. The two of them chased each other round the stage and into the audience.

"I kind of like them this way," said Jo as the twins rolled on the ground, grappling with each other.

Constantine burst into the tent, making everyone turn round. He was out of breath and panicky. "Constantine has been robbed!" he shouted. "Need Kirrin kids and furry dog!"

Constable Stubblefield, the officer in charge of Falcongate police station, stood up from where she had been sitting in the middle of the hypnotist's audience. "Excuse me," she demanded, "who's the constable round here?"

Constantine looked flustered. "Of course," he stammered. "Refrigerator-sized constable always welcome . . ."

THE
FAMOUS FIVE'S
SURVIVAL GUIDE

includes
the NEW
Unsolved
Mystery

*Packed with useful information on surviving outdoors and solving
mysteries, here is the one mystery that the Famous Five never managed
to solve. See if you can follow the trail to discover the location of the
priceless Royal Dragon of Siam.*

The perfect book for all fans of mystery, adventure and the Famous Five!

ISBN 9780340970836

Read the adventures of George and the
original Famous Five in